Dedication

This book is dedicated to two people.

Firstly my Mother Pat Kilburn for bringing up three children on her own and bringing out the best in us all.

R.I.P. Love You Always

Also to my wonderful wife Shirley Kilburn for believing in me.

Once Upon A Time....

In a big house somewhere in Bury, Lancashire, it was a cold and wintery night.

Zofia, Maisie, Joseph and Lucia were all playing in the bedroom when a knock came on the front door. It was Auntie Helen and Uncle David with James.

All the children ran downstairs to meet them.

"Hello Helen, hello James, hello David, said the children. "Hello children"said Helen and David. James went upstairs to play with the others.

Helen was heavily pregnant, she was expecting her second child very soon. David and Helen had joined Christopher and Nicola in the kitchen for a drink. It was a very cold night and it had started to snow heavily. "Oh look at all the snow" said Nicola, " You had better stay for the night".

A Christmas Adventure Story

Helen and David agreed and Helen went upstairs to tell James they were staying the night.

All the children were in Joseph's room looking through the window at the snow falling onto the ground. They all said together ' It will soon be Christmas'! Zofia asked "Who believes in Father Christmas?" Then all the children replied " I think we do, but we have never seen him, shall we go out and play in the snow?" Maisie said she was bored and didn't want to go out into the cold.

All of a sudden a flash of lightning appeared in the bedroom and there was a big fluffy white cloud with two enormous flying birds that no one had seen before. They were coloured like a rainbow.

Then the birds spoke and said " okay children, jump on this cloud and we will take you somewhere that is magical"!

All the children looked at each other with mouths wide open and big wide eyes!

So they all said together "Shall we? and will we be safe"?

The two enormous birds agreed they would be, so they all climbed onto the big fluffy white cloud and it flew straight out of the window and into the cold snowy sky. The children looked down at all the villages below as they flew through the cold night air on this fluffy white cloud.

They started to descend from the sky and landed in what looked like a forest. As the cloud came to a halt, the children all said " where are we?"

The two big colourful birds said...

Wiki woo-wiki-do, this is what you have to do. You must go into the forest and look for a cottage. Once you have been to the cottage and believe in what you see, we will come back for you.

" What if we don't believe?" asked Zofia. Wiki woo-wiki believe or we will have to leave you here. Then the two birds and the cloud disappeared.

"Oh no! what do we do now?" said James

" well we will have to look for the cottage" said Joseph. Then Lucia shouted "Come this way, I can hear faint music

A Christmas Adventure Story

coming from this direction" and was pointing to a bright orange road.

As the children were walking carefully down the road, Lucia said " Be quiet everyone...can you hear that noise?" Shhhh...its coming from over that hedge."

They all peered over the hedge and looked down onto a very big cottage with smoke coming out of a wobbly chimney. " Shall we go down?" asked Joseph....Oh no!! wait a minute, I have just touched the hedge and when I put my hand to my mouth and cannot

believe its made of jelly!...Strawberry jelly! All the children then had a handful and started to eat it. They were laughing and eating jelly. Then James said "lets go down to the cottage and find out what is in there". Everyone agreed and made their way to the cottage.

As they drew nearer to the cottage, they could hear whirring noises!!! clanking noises!!! and thumping noises!!!

"What on earth is making those noises?" said Zofia and Maisie together.

"We have to get closer" said Lucia and James, but Joseph was already at the corner of the cottage waving frantically. The rest of the children ran to him and one said " What's the matter Joseph?" "Have a taste of this" replied Joseph. "Oh my goodness!! its made of chocolate!!" so the children had a taste and all agreed with Joseph that the cottage was made of chocolate. ..."But wait..look at all these coloured buttons, what are these?" said James.

"Oh Wow!! they are my favourite...
Smarties, this is fantastic!! he shouted"
Every time they ate a piece of
chocolate off the cottage, it grew back
again as if by magic...
The Whirring Sound!!, Clanking Noises!!
and the thumping noises were getting
louder. All the children were sitting in
in the snow on the orange coloured path
with their faces covered in chocolate and
feeling full after eating quite a lot of
chocolate.

The noise was coming from a window which was quite high up on the cottage. Maisie said " How on earth are we going to look through the window?" Then they all looked around for things to climb on . They found seven chopped logs and piled them up against the cottage wall. James had brought the last log and said.. "I am going to be the first one up this make-shift staircase" but as he jumped on to the first one, he fell right through it...and the other children ran over to him and James was laughing out loud. "OMG! this is a chocolate log"!! he said.

All of a sudden, there was a little whirring noise, and as if by magic seven chocolate steps were starting to appear out of the Cottage walls. They They were wide enough for all five children to get on one step. So the children climbed to the top of the steps very gingerly, anticipating what they were going to see through the big frosted window.
As they reached the top Zofia said, "I cannot see through the window", Lucia said "wipe the window with your sleeve". So Zofia did and the view inside became clearer...

Through the window all the Whirring, Clanking, and Thumping noises became clear. There was a lot of little men and women dressed in red tops and green trousers' hammering and screwing all all these toys, dolls, cars, bikes, and thousand's upon thousands of other toys. There was a conveyor belt taking the toys, and putting them into the biggest Red Sack that anyone had ever seen. In one area there was a beautiful Princess doll, with the most beautiful dress which was long, white and purple colours and a soldier dressed in the finest uniform of the day.

There was also in the corner of the Chocolate house two of the biggest chairs that the children had ever seen. On the first chair was an old lady with a nice round face and smiling, she was stoking the fire and shouted "Santa it's nearly time to go, come and have your tea". All of a sudden this huge man appeared from a room in the back of the Chocolate house. He was wearing a pair of red pants with black shiny boots and a big red jacket. He had the biggest and best white beard anyone had ever seen.

He walked to the chair to sit next to the old lady. She said "drink your tea. You have a long night ahead."

Meanwhile outside looking through the window Joseph shouted "It's Father Christmas, It's Father Christmas"! Joseph was singing it's 'Father Christmas' and all the other children were singing it's Father Christmas too, Lucia and James were holding hands and swinging round singing it's Father Christmas when all of sudden the cottage window flew open and all the children were lifted into the air and through the window of the Chocolate cottage.

They all floated down in front of the two people sat in the chairs. The old lady said "hello children, it's nice to see you you all" and all the children said together in a shaky voice "Hello". Then little Joseph said shyly "excuse me but are you Father Christmas? " pointing at the old man with Red trousers on. A big booming laugh came from the Old man "Okay children sit down and tell me why you are here?". Zofia said "I am sorry it was my fault because I had asked the other children if they believed in Father Christmas and we were all unsure. Ho Ho Ho...Boomed Father Christmas,

Of course I am real! Ho Ho Ho...
And with that the old Lady took all the
the children and showed them how they
made everyone's Christmas day special.
The children first ran to where they had
seen the Princess and the soldier and
said to the old lady, " We really like these
two toys" and the old lady replied " Yes
they are very special indeed." then with
one loud clap of her hands the princess
doll came to life and spoke "hello" my
name is Abbie ", then the soldier started
marching around and said "Hello I am
Michael" then the old lady said"thank you
Abbie and Michael"and the dolls went
went back into their original postions.

The old lady said they are our two best dolls ever. They have been here a long time and will only go to a house where all children believe. All the children came back to the fire, where Father Christmas was sitting in the chair. All the children with one voice said "we are sorry for not believing" and Father Christmas stopped them talking and said. "There are many thousands of children that don't believe, but you five Children had a little belief that I was real and this is where your adventure started.

James said " Father Christmas, is it true you know the names of all the children in the world?" "Of course I do, James Joseph, Zofia, Maisie, and little Lucia. Now it is time for you to go home as I will be round at your house in a few hours" said Father Christmas. "We are waiting for the Rainbow birds and the big Fluffy white cloud to come and take us home Father Christmas" said the children. Then the old lady said to Father Christmas, " are all the reindeers ready for the off?" "Yes we have all of them tonight, Dasher, Dancer, Prancer,

Vixen, Comet, Cupid, Donner and Blitzen. and Rudolph". Rudolph was the Red nosed Reindeer. "Why do you ask Mrs Christmas?" .."Well we can tell the two Rainbow birds not to come and the children can have a ride home in the spare sleigh and let Atlas the Reindeer fly them home". she said. Good idea said Father Christmas and he shouted "Atlas come to me" then bells were ringing in an instant and outside the Chocolate cottage was Atlas the Reindeer, with a big sleigh to take the children home.

As the children gathered outside they all turned to Father Christmas and Mrs Christmas and said "bye bye and thankyou, we do believe". Then Atlas said "come on... hop in the sleigh" Oh!!!! my goodness Atlas can talk, said Maisie."Of course I can" said Atlas. Zofia, James, Joseph, and Lucia said this is fantastic... a talking Reindeer! As the children sat in the sleigh, it went.... Whooosh!!!!! and up into the night sky. All the Children were looking down and waving to Father and Mrs Christmas.

As they were flying, they went past a Super moon, So big they could nearly touch it. Joseph said to Atlas, "Grandad Mike said the moon was made of cheese he is so silly".

Atlas replied "Grandad Mike is right Joseph let me show you". As Atlas landed on the moon, The man who lives on it said I suppose you would like some Cheese then children. "Yes please" said, Zofia , Maisie, Joseph, James and Lucia. So the man who lives on the moon cut into the moon's surface and gave all the children a slice of cheese.

Then Whoosh!!! Atlas soared back into the air. As they were getting nearer home they saw an ambulance outside the house. "Oh what is going on" said James worriedly. Atlas swooped and landed in the garden. The children got out and said goodbye to Atlas. Then Atlas disappeared into the night sky. All the children ran into the house and Christopher and Nicola said to them all, "did you enjoy playing in the snow?" "Yes" replied all the children. Why is the ambulance outside?" Christopher said " I think you had better go into the back bedroom.....

"Okay Dad, but what is the matter"? said all the children. " Just go into the back bedroom and all will be revealed" he replied. So all of the children opened the door of the back bedroom very slowly. As the door eventually opened, Helen was lying on the bed holding a blanket and David was stood there holding her hand with a big beaming smile. He said " Kids, come in. James I want you to meet your new Sister Grace" and as Helen went to show Grace to the children they all smiled and James had the biggest smile of all of them. She was so beautiful and had a fantastic head of hair!

Zofia , Maisie , Joseph , James, and Lucia said quietly together, "I wonder when Grace gets older, if she will believe in Father Christmas" and with that baby Grace opened her eyes and with one eye, winked at all of the children. Then Maisie went and looked out of the window her eyes and mouth wide open.. As down in the snow was Princess Abbie and Michael the soldier laying there.

Another adventure for another day!

The End

Inspiration

I was inspired to write this book by my Grandchildren and wanted to write a book that included them all.

Acknowledgements

Thanks to Carol Ann Whittle, who without her experience and illustrations, this book would still be in my mind.

Printed in Great Britain
by Amazon